IN THE HAUNTED HOUSE

There was more spooky laughter, but I knew it was just another recording. Haunted houses are really kind of boring. They try to scare you with all this fake stuff, but it never works.

I came to another corner. Just as I turned, I felt something grab my arm. It was a hand.

At first I thought the hand was fake—like everything else—but then the fingers squeezed me, and I knew it was real!

I screamed really loud. And I swung my leg and kicked hard with my foot. My sneaker hit something. It felt bony, like a knee.

Then a dry, scratchy voice cried, *"Erk!"*

THERE'S A TROLL IN MY POPCORN

by Carol Ellis

Illustrated by Pat Porter

A BYRON PREISS BOOK

A MINSTREL® BOOK

PUBLISHED BY POCKET BOOKS

New York London Toronto Sydney Tokyo Singapore

F
ELL

6371

A MINSTREL PAPERBACK *ORIGINAL*

 A Minstrel Book published by
POCKET BOOKS, a division of Simon & Schuster Inc.
1230 Avenue of the Americas, New York, NY 10020

Copyright © 1994 by Byron Preiss Visual Publications, Inc.
Cover artwork copyright © 1994 by Ted Enik.

Special thanks to Ruth Ashby.

Developed by Byron Preiss
Executive Editor: Wendy Wax
Editorial Assistant: Vicky Rauhofer
Illustrations by Pat Porter
Typesetting by Jackson Typesetting Company

ISBN: 0-671-87162-5

First Minstrel Books printing April 1994

10 9 8 7 6 5 4 3 2 1

A MINSTREL BOOK and colophon are registered trademarks of Simon & Schuster Inc.

Printed in the U.S.A.

Chapter 1

Monroe's Mess-Ups

Monroe's Mess-Ups
Better run,
'Cause Winslow's Winners
Are number one!

It was Wednesday. My best friend Sarah and I had just gone outside for recess when we heard a bunch of Winslow kids yelling about Monroe's Mess-Ups. There are two third-grade classes in our school, Ms. Monroe's and Mrs. Winslow's. Sarah and I are in Ms. Monroe's.

"Not again!" I said. "If I hear that stupid chant one more time, I'm going to be sick."

"Be sick by the swings," Sarah said, pointing. "That's where Winslow's class is."

When we got to the swings, a boy in Winslow's class jumped out at us. It was Luis. He's

1

fat, with a short crewcut and a big mouth. "Hey, Annie," he said. "How does it feel to be with a bunch of losers?"

I crossed my eyes and stuck my tongue out at him. Sarah said, "Wait till Friday, Luis, then *you'll* know!"

Luis laughed. "Fat chance, Freckles!"

Sarah has curly red hair and lots of freckles. She hates that nickname. "You better stop stuffing your face, Luis," she said. "You'll have to waddle through all the races on Friday."

Friday was Field Day, and this year was going to be the best one yet. We always have games and food and stuff like that. Only this year the school had rented a small Ferris wheel, a merry-go-round, and a haunted house, just like at a carnival.

Of course we have contests on Field Day. Classes in the same grade compete in relay and sack races and tugs-of-war. Everybody in the winning class gets a trophy and a coupon for a free ice-cream cone.

My class really wanted to win. There was just one problem—anytime there's a contest, Mrs. Winslow's class beats ours. They'd already won trophies for the third-grade spelling bee, the Giant Sneaker for running the most laps around the field, and the Golden Bookmark for the most books read. Field Day was

2

our last chance to win anything before school was out for the summer.

I stuck my tongue out at Luis again. Then Sarah and I ran over to the monkey bars. Lots of the kids from our class were there already. Jason was lying on top of the bars. He's tall, with plain brown hair, like mine. Sam, who has curly black hair, was on a middle rung. Maria, the shortest kid in our class, was sitting on a low bar. Kelly was standing next to her, combing her long, dark hair. Sarah and I sat on the low bars, too.

"Hey, Annie," Jason called down. "What was Luis yelling at you?"

"He asked me what it feels like to be with a bunch of losers," I said.

Maria sighed, her big brown eyes sad. "I wish we'd win something, just once," she said.

"Maybe a bunch of the Winslow creeps will get sick Thursday night," Sam said. He stuck his finger in his mouth and made gagging sounds.

"Don't be so gross," Kelly told him. "Anyway, Mrs. Winslow's class is the one with losers in it. Just look at Dawn."

Dawn was with the rest of her class, over by the swings. She has curly blond hair and wears pierced earrings. That day they were little gold hearts. "Dawn thinks those earrings are *so*

cool," Kelly said. "But I can tell they're not real gold." She climbed a rung of the monkey bars and yelled, "Winslow's class will wimp out! Winslow's Wimps! Winslow's Wimps!"

Dawn stuck her nose in the air and turned her back on us. Other Winslow kids started shouting, "Monroe's Mess-Ups."

Jason stood on top of the bars and yelled back. Maria sighed again. Kelly stomped over to one of the playground monitors to complain that the Winslow kids were being mean.

Sarah and Sam and I walked across the baseball field to where the rides were. The merry-go-round was still on a truck, and workers were busy setting up the Ferris wheel. The haunted house was being tested, and the mechanic had just ducked around the corner of it.

The front of the haunted house was black, with skeletons and ghosts and monster faces painted on it. Spooky music was playing, and a deep recorded voice kept saying, "Don't be frightened. Come inside. Ha, ha, ha!"

Sam ran up the wooden steps and stopped in front of the entrance. It was a hole painted like a wide-open vampire mouth with bloody fangs. "This is seriously scary!" he said. He took a deep breath, then ducked inside.

Sarah grinned at me. "Come on, Annie," she

said. "Let's sneak up on him and give him a *real* scare!" She loves to tease people.

Sarah ran after Sam, and I decided to follow her, even though I knew we shouldn't go in while they were testing the house.

It was dark inside. For a few seconds I couldn't see a thing. Then something white started glowing up ahead. I told myself not to be scared. Haunted houses are never as frightening as they're supposed to be. I held my hands out in front of me and walked down the narrow passage. Suddenly the white thing made a loud rattling sound and jumped out in front of me. I jumped, too. Then I laughed. It was just a plastic skeleton.

The skeleton slid back on its pulley, and I kept walking. I heard Sam yell and Sarah laugh. She must have scared him, I thought. They were way ahead of me so I couldn't see them.

As I turned a corner, something brushed across my face. It was a spiderweb, with a giant spider in it. The spider's legs were moving, but I could tell it wasn't real anyway.

As I kept walking a squeaking sound started over my head. There were bats above me. But they were rubber. I could even see the strings that were holding them.

There was more spooky laughter, but I knew

it was just another recording. I wasn't scared, not even a little bit. Haunted houses are really kind of boring. They try to scare you with all this fake stuff, but it never works.

I came to another corner. Just as I turned, I felt something grab my arm. It was a hand.

At first I thought it was fake—like everything else—but then the fingers squeezed me, and I knew it was real!

CHAPTER 2

TULA'S BACK!

I wasn't bored anymore. I was *seriously* scared!

I screamed really loud. And I swung my leg and kicked hard with my foot. My sneaker hit something. It felt bony, like a knee.

Then a dry, scratchy voice cried, *"Erk!"*

I'd heard that word before, and I knew that voice, too. It belonged to Tula.

Tula is a troll.

"Tula?" I said. "Is that you?"

"Great greedy ogres, Annie!" the voice said. "You should have told me that humans sometimes greet their friends with a kick! When I was here before, I would have learned tofu!"

"Kung fu," I said with a laugh. Now I was sure it was Tula, even though I couldn't see her. She knows our language, but sometimes mixes up the words.

Then a glowing red light came on in the passage and I *did* see Tula.

Tula is short, with green eyes and chipmunk cheeks. She had on a baggy jumpsuit, with orange, green, and blue stripes. She has two arms and legs, but only four fingers and toes on each hand and foot. Her hair is long and shaggy. It's also as pink as cotton candy.

The first time I saw her was in the mess in my closet. I was trying to find my aluminum-foil crown to wear for our class play tryouts. Instead, I found Tula. She had been dying to visit the human world, so she said some magic words and appeared in my closet. She had trouble remembering how to get back to the Land of the Trolls, so she stayed with me for two whole weeks. It was a crazy visit.

"Tula, I'm really glad to see you!" I said. "How are you?"

"Dreadful!" Tula said.

"Oh, no! What's wrong?"

"What's wrong?" Tula cried, peering around. Another skeleton hung at the end of the passage. The recorded voice was still laughing its spooky laugh. "How can you ask such a question, Annie! Doesn't this place fill you with dread?"

I giggled. "It's just a pretend haunted house. I wasn't scared until you grabbed me—that's

why I kicked you. And anyway, I thought you'd come back through my closet," I said.

"I did," Tula said. "But you weren't in your room, and I looked all around your house. . . ."

"Uh-oh," I said. "I hope you stayed invisible." Because I was the first human to see Tula, I will always be able to see her. But nobody else can, unless she goofs and becomes visible. She goofed when she was here before, and my teacher almost fainted!

"Of course I stayed invisible," Tula said. "I can control my magic much better now. When I didn't find you, I came to the school, and I saw this place. I was curious, so I came in." She gasped as the recorded laugh boomed out again. "What a mistake I made!"

"Don't worry," I said. "Everything in here is fake. This haunted house is for Field Day."

"Fielday?" Tula frowned. "Sunday, Monday, Tuesday— Annie, did humans add another day while I was gone?"

I giggled again. I was just about to explain Field Day when I heard footsteps. "Tula, you *are* invisible, right?" I asked quickly.

"Of course," she said. "I think."

"You *think*?"

Just then Sarah came running up. I held my breath. If Tula was visible, Sarah would be able to see her. When Sarah didn't say anything about the pink-haired troll by my side, I let my breath out.

"What's taking you so long, Annie?" Sarah said, laughing. "Sam thought a ghost grabbed you."

"Nothing grabbed me," I said. Except a troll, I thought. "I was just looking around."

The last time Tula was here, I wanted to tell Sarah about her. Maybe this time I would, but not here. Sarah might think it was a trick.

"Recess is almost over," Sarah said. "Come see the big vampire up ahead!"

"*Vampire*," Tula said. "Monster. Fiend. Bloodsucker. *Erk!*"

"Fake," I reminded her.

"Well, sure it's fake," Sarah said. She thought I was talking to her. "But it really scared Sam! Come on!"

I let Sarah get ahead of me. Then I turned to Tula. "Sarah and I are going into the school," I whispered. "You stay outside." Last time she came to school with me, Harry, the class hampster, went bonkers. Animals can always see trolls, and they don't like them.

"All right, Annie," Tula said. "I'll go exploring. I'll meet you at the front door after school."

"Okay, but stay invisible," I hissed at her.

Sarah turned around and stared at me. "Annie, are you starting to talk to yourself again?"

I shook my head. "I said you're almost invisible. It's so dark and everything." The last time Tula was here, people thought I talked to myself a lot. This time I'd try to keep my lips locked.

When we got back to the classroom, it was D.E.A.R. time. That means Drop Everything And Read. We can read anything except comic books. That day, I couldn't concentrate. I kept thinking about Tula. I was happy to see her, but I couldn't help wondering whether she'd cause me any trouble like she did the first time she was here. She had ridden a skateboard into the cafeteria and almost crashed into the principal. People were still talking about the "ghostly" skateboarder.

The more I remembered, the more nervous I got. What would Tula do this time?

"Psst! Annie!" Jason, who sits next to me, poked me in the arm. "Look outside," he whispered. "The Ferris wheel's running now."

I gazed out the window and saw the big wheel slowly spinning. Ms. Monroe left the room for a minute.

"One of the cars has a dragon painted on it," Jason said. "Here, look through this." He handed me a little telescope.

Jason was right. There was a green dragon painted on one of the cars.

There was also a pink-haired troll *in* the car.

The car was swaying, and Tula's hair was flapping in the wind. Her eyes were closed real tight. Hang on, Tula, I thought.

"This is reading time, everybody," Ms. Monroe said, coming back into the room. "Annie Gibson, give Jason his telescope."

I handed Jason the telescope and picked up my book. Then I noticed Sarah giving me a funny look. "What?" I said.

"Your eye," she whispered, giggling. "Your eye has a purple ring around it. You look like somebody punched you."

I turned to Jason. He was pretending to read, but his book was upside-down. His shoulders were shaking, and he kept making little snorting noises.

Ms. Monroe was writing spelling words on the board, her back to us. I reached over and snatched the telescope out of Jason's desk. The eyepiece still had purple ink on it.

"Gotcha!" Jason said. His brown eyes sparkled as he laughed out loud. Ms. Monroe whirled around and frowned at him. He told her his book was really funny.

Jason's always playing dumb practical jokes. On Monday he sprinkled tiny bits of tan paper on Sarah's desk and told everyone her freckles were falling off. Then he tied one of Sam's shoelaces to his chair leg and put a rubber spider in Maria's lunchbox. On Tuesday he told Kelly she had something green stuck on her front tooth. She spent an hour trying to talk without moving her lips. Now he'd gotten me.

As soon as I could, I went to the bathroom and washed the purple ink off my eye. When I got back to class, everybody was staring out the window again. Ms. Monroe walked over to lower the shades. Before she finished, I was able to see what was happening. The merry-go-round was running.

I also saw something nobody else could see—Tula was riding one of the horses. I secretly wished I could tell her to become visible for just a second. I'd make Jason look, and right after he saw her, I'd tell her to disappear. He'd never figure it out.

When school was over, Tula was waiting outside for me. On the way home she kept bumping into me.

"What's wrong with you?" I asked.

"I am still dizzy, Annie," she said. "That purple horse couldn't run straight."

I laughed. "That was the merry-go-round," I told her. Then I explained about carnival rides and Field Day. "We only have to stay in class until ten o'clock. Then we have Field Day outside until two o'clock. Then we clean up and go home. It's a really fun day."

"I am so glad!" Tula said. "It's the rainy season at home. That's why I decided to visit you. We have to stay in our caves most all the time, and I was bored rigid."

"Stiff," I said.

"Exactly," Tula said. "I sneaked out when everybody was asleep. But I have to be back before they wake up."

I remembered that troll time is different than human time. At least that's what Tula says. "Is that long enough for you to be here for Field Day?" I asked Tula. "It's Friday—two human days away."

She started counting on her stubby fingers. "I *might* have just enough time, Annie!" she said excitedly.

"Great," I said. "But remember, Tula, you have to remain invisible."

Tula frowned and her face wrinkled up. "I told you I can control my magic better, Annie." She was insulted. "After all, I'm older now."

Just then Ralph came racing up to the front fence of the Watsons' house, which is next door to mine. Ralph is a dog, a Saint Bernard. I guess he remembered Tula from the last time because as soon as he saw her, he started barking.

"Watch this, Annie!" Tula yelled. She

pointed a stubby finger at Ralph and shouted, *"Zerbit!"*

Ralph stopped barking and wagged his tail.

The last time it took Tula three tries before she remembered the right troll command for "hush and be good."

"You see?" Tula said to me. "I got it right the first time." She reached into a pocket of her jumpsuit and pulled something out. "Look, Ralph," she said. "I brought you a present from the Land of the Trolls."

She dropped something square and white into the yard. Ralph ran up and sniffed it.

"Is it ogre meat?" I joked. There are ogres in the troll world. Trolls are scared of them.

"Ha," Tula said. "Not even dogs will eat ogre meat. It's a Spider Rib. Made from the finest webs in the land of the trolls. The dogs at home really hog out on them."

Ralph "hogged" out on it, too. Then he jumped up on the fence and looked as if he was grinning. Tula patted his head. Ralph put his paws on her shoulders and licked her face. Then he trotted off to the backyard.

"I should have brought more ribs," Tula said, wiping her face.

"You should have brought more clothes," I said. "Look, your outfit has a thousand dog hairs on it."

"A thousand? You must be *flopping* math, Annie." Tula brushed some of the hair off. "There are only sixty-four."

I stared at her. "How do you know that?"

"When trolls are touching things, they can tell exactly how many there are," Tula said. "I just learned this special troll skill. It's called close encounters." She grinned. "Close en*coun-ters*—do you grab it?"

"Get it," I said. "I guess I do, sort of."

We went into my house. My mom was in the kitchen, talking on the phone. I waved and grabbed a handful of chocolate-chip cookies. Cookies are Tula's favorite human food. Last time she ate almost all the oatmeal cookies in the house.

By the time we got to my room, Tula had gobbled down three cookies. "Even better than oatmeal," she said. She was about to put a fourth cookie in her mouth when my little brother jumped out of my closet. Bobby's three, and he likes the closet because I keep my stuffed animals in there.

"Hi, Annie," Bobby said. He started to say something else, but stopped. His eyes opened wide, and so did his mouth. He pointed. I looked.

Bobby was pointing at the cookie Tula was about to eat. Except he couldn't see Tula. All he could see was a cookie floating through the air.

18

Chapter 3

The Ogre Team

The last time Tula was here, she goofed and became visible in front of Bobby. When he saw her, he shrieked. Then, when she was *in*visible, she'd swiped a piece of his toast. I guess he could tell from the floating cookie that she was back. And I just knew he was going to shriek again.

Bobby took a deep breath and opened his mouth even wider. "Tula!" he shouted. He wasn't scared, though. He was shouting because he was excited.

Tula chomped up the cookie. "He can say my name now," she said to me. "Last time he called me 'Tuwa.'"

"Tula!" Bobby shouted again.

"Quiet!" I told him. I didn't want my mother to wonder what was happening.

"Tula!"

"Okay, okay," I said. I looked at Tula. "You might as well become visible," I told her. "Maybe he'll shut up if you do."

I closed the door, and Tula snapped her fingers. Bobby smiled at her. "Are you a clown?" he asked.

"*Clown.* Joker. Fool. Buffoon." Tula frowned at him. "Do I look like a fool?"

"That's not what he means," I told her. "He means a clown in a circus." Actually, she did look a little like a clown in her striped outfit. "A circus clown makes people laugh. And there are going to be kids dressed up as clowns on Field Day, too," I explained. "Bobby loves clowns."

"Want to play hide-and-seek?" Bobby asked Tula.

"No!" I said. "Listen, Bobby, you can't play with Tula while she's here. Except with me, in my room. With the door closed."

"Why?"

"Because I said so," I told him. "You can't tell Mom and Dad about her, either. And if you don't mind me, I won't let you see her anymore. Promise?"

Bobby nodded. Even though he was older now, I wasn't sure I could trust him. But I didn't have much choice.

"What's hide-and-seek?" Tula asked.

After I explained the game, Tula wanted to play. She was really good, because every time it was her turn to hide, she snapped her fingers and made herself invisible. Then she'd move to another place and appear again. I was afraid Bobby would get mad, but he just laughed. He thought Tula was the greatest hide-and-seek player ever.

At dinner Bobby told my parents about the game.

"I'm glad you played with him, Annie," my dad said to me.

"Tula played, too," Bobby said.

"That's nice." Dad smiled. "Who's Tula?"

I tried to kick Bobby under the table. I missed.

"My friend," Bobby said.

"That's nice," Dad said again. "Where does she live?"

Bobby shrugged. "Tula's funny. She has pink hair. And she can disappear."

Dad was frowning now. I tried to kick Bobby again, but I still missed. Then Mom said, "I think someone has an imaginary friend. He's the right age for it."

"Ah!" Dad said. "Well, that explains it."

I was glad *some*body had explained it, because I never could have.

21 ST. GERTRUDE SCHOOL
400 E. CAESAR
KINGSVILLE, TEXAS 78363

*   *   *

The next morning Tula and I walked to school together. We'd gone about a block when I heard footsteps running up behind us. I turned back and saw Luis and Tim from Mrs. Winslow's class.

"Hi, loser!" Tim called. He's chubby, like Luis, and he wears his hair in a crewcut, too.

"Well, well," I said. "If it isn't the Two Stooges."

"Oh, yeah?" Luis laughed. It sounded like a car horn. "A Monroe Mess-Up is calling us stooges?" He snorted. "Your class couldn't win if you were the only class in the contest!"

"Very funny," I said. "So funny I forgot to laugh."

Luis snorted again, and he and Tim ran on. I could hear them shouting the dumb chant about Monroe's Mess-Ups even after they were out of sight.

"Who were those beastly boys?" Tula asked. She sounded mad.

I glanced at her. She was mad, all right. When trolls get angry, their faces turn green, and Tula's was as green as a pickle.

"Luis and Tim," I said. "They're in the other third-grade class." Then I told her about the Field Day contests. "Don't you have contests in the Land of the Trolls?"

"Oh, yes," Tula said. "My favorite is the mushroom hop."

"You hop over mushrooms?" I asked. "That doesn't sound very hard."

"It is when the mushrooms are three feet high," Tula said. "And last season my team lost to the Ogres."

"Ogres!" I said. "I thought you were scared of ogres."

"We didn't play the real ones," Tula said. "That's just what we called the other team because they were so beastly to us. They called us Hop-Floppers." The green was fading from her face, but she still sounded a little mad. "Luis and Tim would be perfect Ogres."

I laughed. "They sure would." We were almost at school now. "Listen, Tula," I said. "Remember to stay in the reading corner in class. Stay invisible. Don't talk to me. And don't go anywhere near Harry the hampster."

"Don't worry, Annie," Tula said. "Nobody will even guess I am there."

I had just about decided to tell Sarah about Tula, but Sarah was absent with a cold.

"She better be back tomorrow," Jason said. "We need everybody if we want to beat Winslow's class."

"And Sarah's in charge of our equipment, too," Kelly said.

Lots of kids had jobs for Field Day. Some would help in the booths. Some would dress up like clowns and hand out balloons to all the little kids who came with their parents. And one person from each grade was in charge of the equipment for the races. Another school had loaned us some of its equipment, so every grade had a different color rope for the tug-of-war, and their own batons and sacks for the sack and relay races. Sarah was in charge of the third-grade equipment. She'd have plenty of free time, though. All she really had to do was bring the stuff out to the field.

"She'll be here tomorrow," I told Kelly and Jason. "Sarah wants to win as much as everybody else does. She won't miss Field Day."

After math we usually have art and then gym. But that day we went outside to help decorate the booths. Mrs. Winslow's class did, too. And so did Tula.

We'd only been outside for two minutes when Luis, Dawn, and Tim started bragging.

"Umm!" Tim said, rubbing his stomach. "I can already taste my ice-cream cone. Chocolate-chocolate chip, that's what I'm going to get."

"What you're going to get is fat," Jason told him.

Dawn gave Kelly a fake smile. "I've got the perfect place for my trophy," she said. "I'll put it on my bookshelf, right next to the one I got for the spelling bee."

"I've got a better idea, Dawn." Kelly tossed her hair back. "If you win, why don't you poke two more holes in your ears and wear the stupid trophies?"

"Thanks for the advice," Dawn said. "But don't you mean *when* I win?"

"She's on the Ogre team," Tula muttered.

"Right," I said.

Jason and Kelly and the others stared at me. They thought I was agreeing with Dawn. "I mean, *Kelly's* right, Dawn," I said. "Anyway, why don't you guys get lost?"

"Mushroom Heads," Tula grumbled. "Hop-Floppers."

"Mushroom Heads. Hop-Floppers," I said to the Winslow kids.

"They've got moss for brains," Tula said.

"Right, you've got moss for brains," I said.

"Moss for brains?" Jason said. He laughed. "I like that one." He turned to the Winslow kids and started calling them Moss-for-Brains and Mushroom Heads and Hop-Floppers. Soon, we were all calling them troll names.

Then Ms. Monroe and Mrs. Winslow told us to be good sports and get to work.

I headed for the fortune-telling booth. Kids from different grades were going to take turns being the fortune-teller, and Ms. Monroe had picked me to be one of them. I'd have three turns. I'd get to wear a turban and makeup and lots of silky scarves. I couldn't wait.

Some parents had built the fortune-telling booth out of wood a few years ago. It was painted black, with silver and gold stars and moons. Ms. Monroe asked me to paint the sign. On the way to the booth Tula and I passed a big, see-through bin filled with popcorn.

"Snow, correct?" Tula said.

"Wrong," I said. "It's popcorn. Food."

"Excellent!" Tula said. "I am awesomely hungry."

Before I could stop her, she ran over to the bin and grabbed a handful of popcorn. I ran after her, but I was too late. She'd already stuffed the popcorn into her mouth.

"Delicious!" she said.

"We're not supposed to eat it!" I told her.

"Who's eating it?" Sam asked. He was walking toward us, carrying a hammer.

"Uh, nobody," I said. "I was just telling myself not to eat any popcorn. I'm starved."

I waited until Sam was gone. "It's for the contest," I whispered to Tula. "Whoever comes

closest to guessing how many pieces of popcorn are in the bin wins points for their class."

Tula finished chomping the popcorn. "Sorry,
Annie."

"Well, don't eat any more," I said. "The
teachers counted it when they put it in there.
I just hope nobody notices that some pieces
are missing."

"Not *some* pieces," Tula said. "Fifty pieces."

"Fifty? You mean you counted them?" I
asked.

"No, I *ate* them," Tula said. "Trolls eat to
learn, don't you remember?"

"Oh, right. How could I forget?" I said. "The
last time you were here, you ate my list of
spelling words."

"Yes," Tula said. "They weren't as tasty,
though. Especially *dinosaur*. Very tough."

"What about close encounters?" I asked.
"That's how you counted the dog hairs."

"Well, of course," Tula said. "I wouldn't *eat*
dog hairs, Annie. Trolls use close encounters
for things they can't eat, or when there is too
much to eat. Like the popcorn. I could eat all
the popcorn to count it, but then I would be
awesomely ill."

We kept walking and passed the hot dog
booth. *"Hot Dogs,"* Tula read. She frowned.
"Heated canines?"

"Hot dogs are food, too," I told her.

Tula's eyes got real wide. "And humans *eat* them?"

I laughed. "They're not really dogs," I said. "They're called that because they're long and round, like a Dachshund. That's a real dog, but hot dogs are just sort of a sandwich. I bet you'll love them."

"As much as cookies?" Tula asked.

"Maybe not," I said. I didn't think anybody liked anything as much as Tula liked cookies.

Just before we got to the fortune-telling booth, Jason ran up to me. "Hey, Annie, I liked the names you called the Winslow kids," he said. "Got any more?"

"Ogre breath," Tula told me.

"Sure," I said to Jason. "How about ogre breath?"

"Great!" He laughed and kept on running.

When Tula and I got to the fortune-telling booth, I laid my piece of poster board on a bench and knelt down to make the sign. I opened my poster paints and was just starting to draw a fat red *F* when somebody smacked me in the back.

I went sprawling forward onto the bench, and my fat red *F* turned into a fat red blob.

CHAPTER 4

MADAM SHASTA KNOWS ALL

"Hey!" I yelled. "Who did that?" It had to be somebody from Mrs. Winslow's class.

I stood up and looked for Luis, or Dawn, or Tim. All I saw was Tula.

"Tula, did you see who hit me?" I asked.

"Not exactly," she said. "But I know who it was."

"Who?"

"Me!" Tula's eyes squinched up and she made a sound like squeaky bedsprings. She was laughing.

"You?" I said.

Tula nodded and kept squeaking.

"But why?" I asked. "Why'd you do that?"

"I will show you," she said. I felt her stubby hands on my back. Then I heard a crackling sound. Tula held up a piece of paper. "This was stuck on your back," she said.

I grabbed the paper. It said, "HIT ME!"

"Why do you look so mad, Annie?" Tula asked. "I was just following instructions. And I didn't hit you very hard."

"I know." I wadded the paper up and threw it in a trash barrel. "You fell for one of Jason's practical jokes," I said. Then I told her about all the tricks Jason had been playing lately.

"Are these jokes a special thing for Field Day?" Tula asked.

"No, they're a special thing for Jason," I said. I studied the poster board. One side was ruined, but the other side was fine. I painted the words *Fortune-Teller* in red, then I took a yellow marker and drew stars around the words. I stepped back to admire my sign. "What do you think?" I asked Tula.

"*Fortune.* Treasure. Gold," Tula said. She looked around. "Where?"

"It's not that kind of fortune," I told her. "A fortune-teller predicts the future."

"Impossible!"

I laughed. "Some people believe in it, but we're just doing it for fun," I told her. "I'll try to say things that might come true. Like, I'll tell Sam I see tears in his future. His mom's having a baby, and babies always cry."

"What will you tell Jason?" Tula asked.

"I don't know yet," I said. "But I'll think of

something to pay him back for that joke. He needs something extra special in his future."

Tula grinned. "And I can help you, Annie."

Finally Field Day arrived. Before I went to school, I put on my fortune-teller "face" with Mom's makeup. I drew a big black mole on my cheek. Tula watched me closely. Then she said she wanted to wear makeup, too.

"You don't need any," I told her. "You're going to be invisible, remember?"

"I know, but I want to paint my face, too. It will be fun." Tula's face wrinkled.

"Oh, all right," I said and gave her the makeup. First, Tula put powder all over her face. Then she smeared a ton of green eye shadow on her eyelids. She drew a big red circle on each cheek with the lipstick. With her pink hair and striped outfit, she really looked like a clown!

"I hope I can stay for the whole day, Annie," she said, admiring herself in my mirror.

"I hope you can, too," I said. I really did. Having a troll around was weird, but fun.

Mom drove me to school, because she was going to work in one of the food booths. Lots of parents were. Bobby came, too. He would stay with Mom all day, thank goodness. My little brother could be a pest sometimes.

"Is Tula here?" Bobby kept asking in the car.

Tula was sitting next to him. "If you can't see her, she's not here," I said.

"Annie," Mom said. "Don't tease him about his imaginary friend."

"Imaginary?" Tula said. "Ha!"

"I want to see her!" Bobby said.

"Do you want me to snap my fingers and appear?" Tula asked me.

"No!" I said.

"Annie, for heaven's sake," Mom said. "Don't get in an argument with your little brother. He's just going through a stage."

"I want to see Tula!" Bobby yelled.

Mom sighed. "I just hope this stage doesn't last very long," she said.

When we got to school, Tula and I went to my classroom. When I walked in, Jason said, "Ready to beat the Mushroom Heads, Annie?"

"Mushroom Heads?" Sarah was back and she laughed.

"That's what Annie called Mrs. Winslow's class," Maria said. Almost everybody in our class was wearing shorts and T-shirts, but Maria was in a clown costume. When she wasn't in the races, she'd hand out balloons. She wore a pink wig with an orange stripe down the back, and red circles on her cheeks.

She's so short, she looked almost like Tula's twin! "She called them Hop-Floppers, too," she said.

"And Moss-for-Brains," Jason said.

"Don't forget Ogre-Breath," Tula said to me from the reading corner.

"And Ogre-Breath," I said.

Sarah gave me a thumbs-up. "I never knew you could be so funny, Annie."

"I'm learning," I said. From a troll, I didn't add.

"All right, everybody," Ms. Monroe said. "Let's stop the name calling. Remember, this is just a friendly contest."

"That's what *she* thinks," Jason whispered to me. "This is war."

First, we had to do math, then we had to read. I kept smelling hot dogs and cotton candy and I couldn't concentrate. Finally at ten o'clock, Ms. Monroe handed out our tickets for the booths and said we could go. Everybody cheered and ran outside. Sarah and I walked together, and Tula was right behind us. First came the game booths—a ring toss, penny-pitching for prizes, and lots more. Then we passed the food booths. The rides were at the farthest corner of the ballfield.

"Let's go ride the Ferris wheel!" Sarah said.

"Later," I said. "I tell fortunes for half an

hour." All the fortune-tellers would take turns, and my turn was first.

"Okay. See you at the tug-of-war!" Sarah said and ran off.

All the grades had their races at different times. First came the tug-of-war for the kindergartners, then the first grade's tug-of-war, the second grade's, and so on. The next race would be the wheelbarrow race, then the relay race and the sack race. The last contest was the popcorn count. All day long kids would put their guesses in a box next to the barrel. At the end of the day the winners would be announced.

Tula and I headed for the fortune-telling booth. When we passed the barrel of popcorn, I thought about the fifty pieces of popcorn Tula had eaten. I hoped nobody's guess would be wrong because of the missing pieces.

We came to the hot dog booth, and Tula wanted to try a "heated canine." I ordered two from Kelly, who was working there. *"Two?"* Kelly said. "You'll turn into a blimp, Annie."

"Blimp. Airship. Balloon," Tula said. "Maybe I shouldn't eat it after all."

"It means fat," I told her.

"No kidding," Kelly said to me. "Don't pig out, or you'll be too full to run in the races."

I told Kelly not to worry, and Tula and I left. Just before we got to the fortune-telling booth,

Jason ran past us. "I just got off the merry-go-round!" he said. "I'm so dizzy, I think I'm gonna puke!" Then he ran into the school.

"Puke?" Tula's eyes opened wide. "Uh-oh!"

"Uh-oh is right," I said. "I hope he makes it."

One of the playground monitors was outside the fortune-telling booth. Tula and I went inside. I put on a bunch of silky scarves while Tula gobbled her hot dog. "Not bad," she said. "But you're right, I like cookies better."

I stuck the purple turban over my hair just as Maria came into the booth. "I'm ready to have my fortune told, Annie," she said.

"I'm not Annie." I made my voice low. "I'm Madam Shasta. I can see into your future!"

Maria giggled and sat down on one side of the table. It was covered with a black velvet cloth, and it had a crystal ball in the middle of it. I sat down opposite Maria and put my fingers on the crystal ball. I closed my eyes and rubbed the ball. Then I opened my eyes.

"What do you see?" Maria asked.

"Fingerprints," Tula said.

"Very funny," I told Tula.

"Really?" Maria said. "Something funny's going to happen?"

"Maybe," I said.

"What?" Maria asked.

"Good question," Tula said.

"Quiet," I told her.

"Sorry," Maria said.

I stared at the crystal ball some more. I knew Maria was going to the beach in the summer. "I see you running," I said. "And laughing. Lots of people are with you." Maria's cousins were going, too. "Now you're holding something in your hands."

"What is it?" Maria asked. "Can you see?"

"Not clearly," I said. I hadn't thought of anything yet. Then I remembered that Maria collects seashells. "It's very delicate. You're holding it in your hands so it won't break."

"I know!" Tula said. "It's an egg!"

"It's not smooth," I said. "It's bumpy."

"What is it?" Tula asked.

"I'll tell you later," I said.

"Later?" Maria acted confused.

I gave Tula a dirty look. "The crystal is getting cloudy," I said to Maria. "Look for something fragile and bumpy in your future."

"Well, okay, Annie. I mean, 'Madam Shasta.' " Maria got up and left.

"Tula!" I said. "I can't tell fortunes when you keep jabbering at me."

"But what was the bumpy thing?" Tula asked.

"A seashell! Maria's going to the beach this

summer," I said. "Now lock your lips, somebody else is coming!"

After Maria left, a fourth grader came in. I
didn't know her, so I said I saw a fall in her
future. I meant the season. Then she tripped and
fell on her way out of the booth. What luck!

I got lucky with a kindergartner, too. His
candy apple was about to fall off its stick. I
told him he was going to lose something red
and round. A few seconds after he left, he ran
back into the booth. "My candy apple fell!" he
said, amazed. Tula just giggled. I told him my
mom worked at the booth and she'd give him
another one if he told her what happened.

After a few more fortunes, the monitor told
me it was time for the third-grade tug-of-war.
A boy in the fifth grade took my place in the
booth, and Tula and I went to the field.

Sarah brought our rope, which was still
coiled up, and tossed it down in the dirt. It was
yellow, with a white flag tied at the middle.
Jason started to grab the rope, but Ms. Monroe
waved him away and blew her whistle.

"Are the teams ready?" Ms. Monroe said.

"Yeah, we're ready to watch you guys lose
your first battle!" Luis yelled at us.

"You wish!" Sarah yelled back.

"Yeah, fat chance, Ogre-Breath!" Sam shouted.

There was a long white chalk line drawn in

the dirt. "The team that pulls the white flag across the line wins," Ms. Monroe said. "Now take your places!"

Mrs. Winslow's class hurried to one side of the line, grabbed one end of the rope, and uncoiled it. We lined up on the other side.

"Ready . . ." Ms. Monroe said.

"This is weird," Maria said. She was in front of me. "The rope feels slimy."

"Slimy?" Jason said. He was behind me. "Are you sure?"

"Set . . ." Ms. Monroe said.

"Maria's right," I said. "It's all slippery. What's it made of, anyway?"

"Go!" Ms. Monroe yelled, and blew her whistle.

Everybody started yelling and tugging. I was trying to pull, but my hands kept slipping. Then I felt someone grab on to me from behind. It was Tula. I knew she wanted to help, but I couldn't let her. It would be like cheating, even though nobody knew.

Just as I was about to tell her to let go, the Winslow team gave a giant tug. We all tried to hold on, but the rope slithered through our hands and we went with it, right toward the white line!

CHAPTER 5

WINNERS OR CHEATERS?

Tula fell on top of me. I landed on top of Sam. We all scrambled up real fast. "What happened?" I asked.

"We lost," Sam said, brushing the dust off his yellow T-shirt. "Look."

I checked out the rope. The white flag was over the chalk line, on the Winslow side. Ms. Monroe and Mrs. Winslow congratulated them and then walked off. My team gathered around the rope. The Winslow kids were giving one another high fives.

"We should have won," Jason said.

"All I know is I couldn't hold on to the rope," Maria said. "It was too slippery." She wiped her hands on her clown suit. "My hands still feel kind of slimy."

"Mine, too," Sam said.

We all looked at our hands.

"Yuck!" Kelly wiped her hands on her red shorts. "I can't stand this slimy feeling!"

"It's weird," Sam said. "It's like the rope had grease on it."

"I bet it did!" Kelly said. She whirled around and glared at the Winslow team. "I bet you guys greased it, just so we'd lose!"

Dawn laughed at her. "You were going to lose no matter what," she said. "We didn't have to grease the stupid rope!"

"Yeah, and even if we did, you couldn't prove it," Luis said.

We all stared at the rope. It was covered with dirt. Luis was right. If it had been greased, we wouldn't be able to prove it.

Dawn smiled her fake smile. "Monroe's Mess-Ups better run, 'cause Winslow's Winners are number one!" she said in a sing-song voice. Then all the kids on her team ran off, yelling, "We're number one!" The rest of us just stood and stared at the rope.

Kelly turned to Sarah. "Didn't it feel greasy to you when you put it out?"

"No," Sarah said. "But it was coiled up. All the stuff for the races is kept in the same tent. It would have been easy for one of Winslow's team to go in there and grease the rope. It wasn't my job to stand guard over it, you know."

"Well, maybe you should have," Kelly said.

"Look," Jason said. "It's not Sarah's fault."

"Right," I said. "It's the Winslow team's fault. They're the ones we should be mad at."

"Correct," Tula said to me. "They have ogre breath *and* ogre brains. Very sly and tricky."

I couldn't help smiling.

"There's nothing we can do about it now," Sam said. "Let's just win the next one."

It wasn't time for the third-grade wheelbarrow race yet, so we all left. Sarah and I decided to go on the Ferris wheel. Tula wanted to come, too, but there wasn't room for her.

"Let's rock the car," Sarah said as the Ferris wheel started.

"Let's not!" I said. I held the bar tight.

"I didn't know you were scared of heights."

"I'm not," I said.

Sarah laughed. "Then how come your knuckles are white?"

"I guess I *am* scared," I admitted.

"It's okay," she said. "I won't rock the car."

As we went up higher, I closed my eyes. Finally Sarah poked me in the side. "Just take one little peek, Annie. You can see for miles. It's great!"

I took a deep breath and opened my eyes. We were at the very top. I looked down and saw Tula staring up at me. She waved. I let go of the bar with one hand and waved back.

"Who are you waving to?" Sarah asked.

"Oh—just the crowd," I said. I'd have to wait until the three of us were alone together to tell Sarah about Tula.

After the ride Sarah went to the haunted house. I went back to the fortune-teller's booth.

"I will explore while you predict the future, Annie," Tula said.

"Okay, but stay out of sight," I warned. "And don't swipe any food. If you do, people will start talking about ghosts."

Tula promised. I went to the booth and put on the turban and the scarves. Sam came in. I told him to expect tears in three months. His mother was going to have a baby then.

"Three months?" he said. "I don't get it."

"You will!" I told him.

Next I told a second grader that I saw high numbers in her future. Her mom is friends with mine, and she's always bragging about how smart her little girl is in math.

I told two more fortunes. Then Kelly came in. I started rubbing the crystal ball.

"I hope you see gold," Kelly said.

I hadn't even decided what to say to her. But I could make up something gold. "Yes," I said in my deepest voice. "I do see gold."

"Where?" Kelly looked excited.

"In your hand," I told her.

"Hand?" Kelly said. She acted disappointed. "But I was thinking about earrings. I want some, just like Dawn's, but my mom won't let me get my ears pierced."

I dropped my Madam Shasta voice. "You said Dawn's earrings weren't cool!"

"They're not," Kelly said. "Not on *her*."

"Well, I was thinking of the gold ring on the merry-go-round," I said.

"It's brass, not gold. And I hate the merry-go-round." Kelly crossed her arms. "You don't know anything about the future, do you?"

Before I could answer, Tula came running in. "Annie, guess what I did?" She was laughing her squeaky laugh. "I threw a ball, and a girl fell into a big tub of water!"

Tula was talking about the water dump. Somebody sat on a shelf, and somebody else threw a ball at a target. If the target was hit, the person fell into the water.

"And guess who it was?" Tula asked. "That girl from the moss-brain team. Sunrise!"

"Dawn," I said.

"Dawn?" Kelly asked. "What about Dawn?"

I smiled at her. "The picture is changing," I said in my low voice. "The gold has vanished. But I see Dawn clearly. And she's all wet."

"What kind of fortune is that?" Kelly asked.

"You'll see, " I told her.

When my time was up, we went outside. Dawn had just climbed out of the water. A bunch of kids were watching and laughing.

"I don't believe it!" Kelly said. "She's dripping. Who did it?"

"Nobody knows," Sam said. "The ball just came flying out of nowhere."

Tula laughed and poked me in the side. "That's what *he* thinks."

Kelly frowned at me. "How did you know it would happen, Annie?" she asked. She was confused. "We were in the booth!"

I made my voice low again. "Madam Shasta knows all," I said.

Tula laughed and poked me in the side again.

When it was time for the wheelbarrow race, we went back to the field. Dawn had brought a change of clothes, including different earrings. The new ones were little red apples. "Plastic," Kelly said to me with a sniff. She showed me her charm bracelet. "This is real gold," she said. "Not like those cheapo heart earrings Dawn had on before."

"Partners, line up!" Mrs. Winslow yelled.

We all got ready at the starting line. Sarah's

partner was Kelly, Sam and Jason were together, and Maria was my partner. She would
hold my legs up while I ran on my hands. Her
clown costume zipped up the front, and she'd
taken it off. Underneath, she had on green
shorts and a pink T-shirt.

"Get set!" Mrs. Winslow shouted. "Go!"

Maria lifted my legs and we took off. Out of
the corner of my eye, I could see Dawn and
her partner. We were even. "Hurry, Maria!"
I shouted.

"I can't go any faster than you do!" she
shouted back.

I tried to run faster. It was hard because
there were pebbles and sticks and little lumps
of dirt under my hands. And my arms were
getting tired. But Dawn and her partner were
dropping back. Maria and I were ahead!

Suddenly Maria yelled and dropped my legs.
Before I could see what had happened, she
picked them up again. At least, I thought it
was Maria. But when I turned my head, I saw
Tula's pink hair bobbing up and down behind me.

"Tula, no!" I cried. "You're not in the race!"

I guess Tula didn't hear me, because she
kept on running. So I did, too, on my hands.
We didn't stop until we crossed the finish line.
I looked back and saw Maria sitting on the

ground. The two teachers were bending over her, and she was holding her ankle.

I looked at Tula. "You shouldn't have grabbed me!" I muttered.

"Why not?" Tula said. "I wanted to help."

I wanted to yell. I wanted to tell Tula I'd never be able to explain running on my hands by myself. But everybody was gathering around me, so I had to keep my mouth shut.

"How did you do that?" Jason asked me. "You can't even do a handstand!"

"Uh," I said. Jason was right—I can't do a handstand.

"It's impossible," Kelly said. "Nobody can run on their hands like that."

"Well, Annie did it, didn't she?" Sarah said. "Do you think she has invisible strings or something holding her up?"

Just an invisible troll, I thought.

"Okay, but it doesn't count anyway," Luis said. "You have to win with a partner."

"So? Kelly and I won anyway," Sarah told him. "Now we're tied with Winslow's Wimps!"

Everybody on my team forgot about me and started cheering. The Winslow team stood near us, scowling. Tula gave me a thumbs-up sign. At least, I think it was her thumb. It was the shortest of her four fingers. I decided not to yell at her. This time.

Just then Maria came limping up. "Are you okay?" I asked her.

"My ankle's sore, but it's not too bad," she said. She gave me a funny look. "How did you know that was going to happen, Annie?"

"I didn't," I said.

"But you predicted it, remember?" Maria said. "You saw me running with a lot of people. Then you saw me holding something in my hands. Something bumpy that I didn't want to break. Well, that was my ankle!"

"Wow," Sam said.

"And she knew Dawn would get wet, too," Kelly said.

"Madam Shasta knows all," I joked.

Dawn overheard me. She put her hands on her hips. "Well, if you know everything, then you must know our team's going to win the rest of the races," she said. "Right, Annie?"

"Can you really see who'll win, Annie?" Maria asked.

I couldn't, of course, but I didn't want to say that. And I didn't want to predict the wrong thing, either. So I just laughed. "I must consult the crystal ball," I said. "But first, I must eat."

"Again?" Kelly said. "You already had two hot dogs!"

"Don't worry, Kelly," I said. "I'm not a blimp yet!"

Sarah, Sam, Jason, and I left the field and bought snowcones. Jason's fell out of his cup, and he caught it in his hands. Then he had to go into the school to wash up. Tula wanted a snowcone, but I told her she'd have to wait. I didn't want any food floating through the air.

After we finished our cones, we went to the Tower of Strength, where you bang a base with a big hammer to try to make a metal puck slide up a pole and ring a bell. At the top was the word *Hercules*. Sarah got the puck up to Weakling. Sam and I didn't get it past Puny. We were walking away when we heard the bell ring. We all whirled around.

Tula hadn't used the hammer. She'd just jumped onto the base and stomped.

"Awesome!" Sam said. "Did anyone see who did it?"

"Hercules!" Tula shouted, but I was the only one who heard her.

"Weird," Sam said, shaking his head.

As we left the Tower of Strength, a monitor came up and said we should get ready for the relay race. The second graders had just finished theirs, and it was our turn.

We went to the track and got in our places. Sarah had already put the batons on a bench, and I picked one up. I was running first, and I would hand off to Kelly.

The baton felt funny, but I didn't have time to figure out why. Ms. Monroe blew the whistle and I had to start. I held the baton real tight. If I dropped it, I'd really mess things up.

As I raced down the track, I heard Tula shouting at me. She was running along the outside of the track. "Go, Annie!" she yelled.

I ran faster and sped ahead of Jenny, the first runner on the Winslow team. Tula kept up with me, cheering all the way.

When I got close enough to Kelly, I held out the baton. She reached back and I slapped it into her hand, just as they taught us in gym. "Go, Kelly!" I shouted.

Kelly went. But so did I!

"I've got the baton!" Kelly screamed at me. "Let go of it!"

I tried to let go, but my hand wouldn't come loose.

"Let go!" Kelly screamed again.

"I can't!" I screamed back. "I'm stuck!"

Kelly yanked, but it didn't do any good. The two of us were stuck together. The girl from the Winslow team raced ahead, leaving us in the dust.

Chapter 6

Close Encounters

For a couple of seconds Kelly and I kept running together.

"Let go, Annie!" Kelly screamed again.

"I'm trying!" I shouted. "Pull harder!"

Finally Kelly gave a giant tug, and the baton went flying through the air. She picked up a stick from the ground and kept running. But she was so far behind, it didn't matter. Winslow's Winners won the relay race.

After it was over, everybody wanted to know what had happened.

"Annie wouldn't let go, that's what happened," Kelly said.

"I tried to!" I said. "The stupid baton wouldn't come out of my hand."

"What difference does it make?" Luis said. The Winslow kids were slapping hands again. "We were going to win anyway."

Carol Ellis

My team started yelling at Luis's team while I went to look for the baton. I found it in some weeds. I picked it up and tried to wipe it off. The dirt stuck to it, just like it had to my hand.

When I got back to my team, Jason was saying, "We were supposed to win this one. I mean, we're faster than they are!"

"Not today!" Tim said. Luis laughed.

"Look at this," I said to my team. I held out the baton. "Doesn't it look like there was something on it?"

Jason grabbed it out of my hand. "I don't see anything," he said. "Except dirt."

"That's what I mean," I said. "The dirt's all stuck to it, like the baton has glue on it."

Sam took the baton from Jason. "There probably *was* glue on it!" He gave the Winslow team a dirty look.

Luis snorted. "You guys are sore losers, that's all."

"And you guys are cheaters!" Kelly said.

The Winslow team just laughed and ran off.

"I'm sure there was glue on it," I said.

"But it's like the rope," Sam said. "We can't prove anything."

Kelly glared at Sarah. "You're in charge of the equipment. Didn't you notice the glue?"

Sarah gave Kelly a dirty look. "The batons

54

were fine when I brought them out to the field."

"Well, how long did you leave them out there?" Kelly asked.

"I put them on a bench, right before the wheelbarrow race," Sarah said.

"So it happened sometime between the wheelbarrow race and the relay race," Sam said. "I guess there are so many people around, nobody noticed who did it."

"Sarah didn't, that's for sure," Kelly said.

"What do you want me to do, Kelly?" Sarah asked. "Sit out in the field all day?"

"That's a good idea," Kelly said.

Sarah laughed. "Then maybe *you* should do it."

Kelly rolled her eyes.

"Stop blaming Sarah," I said to Kelly. "We know who put glue on the baton. And it wasn't anyone from our class."

"If anybody *did* put glue on it," Jason said. "We can't be sure."

"Well, *I'm* sure," Kelly said. She stomped off.

The rest of us started walking back toward the booths. Suddenly I realized that Tula wasn't with me. I looked around. She wasn't on the Ferris wheel or the merry-go-round. Then I spotted someone with bright pink hair.

"What are you looking for?" Sarah asked.

"Uh—I think I dropped a ticket," I told her. "I'll catch up with you guys in a minute."

I ran toward Tula. But then I saw that it wasn't Tula. It was Maria. She had put her clown costume and wig on again. I ran back to the group, wondering where Tula was. Maybe it was daytime in the Land of the Trolls and she'd had to go back. Wouldn't she have said goodbye, though?

We kept walking until we came to the big bin of popcorn. Next to it was a box with a slit in the top.

Sam took a slip of paper from the table the barrel was sitting on. "I say at least five hundred." He wrote his name and the number down and stuck the paper in the box.

"More than that," Jason said. "A thousand. Maybe two thousand." He wrote down his entry and stuffed it in.

"You're way off," Sarah told them. "Look at the size of that bin. There are at least ten thousand pieces in there. That's what I'm going to guess." She grabbed a slip of paper and wrote her number down.

I was still worried about those fifty pieces of popcorn Tula ate. And I kept wondering where she was. Suddenly Sam said, "Wow. Look at that popcorn! It's bouncing around like crazy!"

I looked at the bin. The popcorn was bouncing, all right. And so was Tula, who was *inside* the barrel. She was trying to climb out. But every time she moved, the popcorn shuffled and jumped around.

"There must be jumping beans in the barrel," Jason said.

"Or else it's haunted," Sam said.

"Maybe Winslow's Weirdos have struck again," Sarah said. Then she laughed. "I guess they couldn't sabotage the popcorn, though."

"They could be counting it," Sam said.

"Inside the barrel?" Sarah stared at him as if he'd gone bonkers. "Do you see anybody inside the barrel, Sam?"

Sam didn't, but I did.

Finally Tula pulled herself out, and the popcorn stopped jumping around.

"Okay, so it was a ghost," Sam said.

"Ever since I scared you in the haunted house, you've had ghosts on the brain," Sarah said. "Come on, it's lunchtime. Let's eat."

The others started for the food booths. I motioned for Tula to come, too. I wasn't hungry, but Tula wanted another hot dog, so I got her one. Kelly was back at the booth, and she stared at me. "That's your fourth one, Annie," she said. "You're really pigging out!"

I pretended not to hear her. When Sarah and

Sam and Jason went to pitch pennies, I told them I needed a drink of water. What I really wanted to do was talk to Tula about jumping in the popcorn. When we got away from the crowded booths, I said, "Next time you decide to go swimming, Tula, do it in a pool."

"I wasn't swimming," she mumbled, chewing her hot dog. "I was counting. I just *had* to find out how many pieces there are, Annie."

"Jumping into the barrel isn't the way to do it," I said.

"It's the troll way!" Tula said. "Close en-*counters*, remember?"

"Okay, okay," I said. Then I realized what she was telling me. "Did it really *work?*"

"Of course it did. There are ten thousand, four hundred and sixty pieces of popcorn in the barrel," Tula said.

I stared at her. "Are you sure?"

"I have never flopped math in my life," Tula said. "Anyway, it was very strange. Right before I jumped into the popcorn, I saw daylight."

"Daylight?" I said. "What do you mean? It's one o'clock in the afternoon. Of course you saw daylight."

"*Nerks*," Tula said. "I got the word mixed up. I meant sunrise."

"Sunrise? Oh," I said, understanding. "You mean Dawn, the girl in Mrs. Winslow's class?"

Tula nodded. "She was standing by the bin with one of the beastly boys, the one with the largest mouth."

"Luis," I said.

Tula nodded again. A piece of popcorn fell out of her hair. She picked it up and ate it. "Correction," she said. "Ten thousand, four hundred and fifty-nine pieces."

"What about Luis and Dawn?" I asked.

"Oh, yes. It was odd. They were talking about glue."

"Glue?" I got excited. "What did they say?"

"Dawn said nobody could see the glue," Tula told me. "I didn't hear what Luis said. Right at that moment I slipped and fell into the barrel."

"I knew it!" I said. "I knew they did it!"

"Did what?"

I told her about the baton.

"Is that why you and Kelly carried the stick between you?" Tula said. "I thought it was part of the game."

"No, it was part of the sabotage," I said. "Just like the grease on the rope."

"*Sabotage.* Damage. Destroy. Ruin," Tula said. Her face started to turn green. "And you think those two did it?" she asked.

"Yes, but it's too late to prove it." I thought a minute. The last two contests were the sack race and the popcorn count. I didn't think Luis and Dawn could do anything about the popcorn. But they might be able to sabotage the sack race.

"Tula," I said. "I have a feeling that Luis or Dawn might do something to the sacks in the sack race. They're the most suspicious ones in Winslow's class. I'm not sure what they'll do, but somebody has to keep an eye on them!"

"You want me to spy?" Tula said.

"Exactly." Tula made a great spy—nobody could see her. "They probably won't be together most of the time, though," I said. "I guess it won't be easy. Just do your best." Then I remembered that she might have to leave. "Will you have time?" I asked.

"I have a few minutes left," Tula said with a grin. "I will begin spying right now!"

We started walking back toward the crowd. On the way we passed the candy apple booth.

"Oh, Annie," Mom said. "Am I glad to see you! Bobby's been stuck in this booth with me all morning. He's starting to go bananas."

"He doesn't look yellow to me," Tula said.

"It's an expression," I told her. "It means crazy."

"I know that, Annie," Mom said. "Anyway,

would you mind taking him with you for a little while? Take him on the merry-go-round and buy him a hot dog."

"I have to go back and tell fortunes," I said. It was my last turn in the booth.

"Well, maybe you could take him with you and tell him his fortune," my mother said. "Tell him you see food and fun in his future."

"I want to ride the merry-go-round," Bobby said. "Now."

"I can't do it now, Bobby," I told him.

"Ask Tula to take me," Bobby said.

"Tula gets too dizzy on it," I said, not thinking.

"I told you not to tease him about that," Mom said.

Tula laughed. But Bobby got mad. His face got pink and he started hopping up and down. "Tula!" he yelled. "Tula, Tula, Tula!"

"Bobby, stop it," Mom said.

Bobby didn't stop. He kept shouting Tula's name over and over. He was so loud, I was embarrassed. My mom leaned her elbows on the counter and put her head in her hands.

"Tula!" Bobby screamed.

"Erk!" Tula said. "Don't worry, Annie, I will make him lock his lips!"

Before I could stop her, Tula raised her hand and snapped her fingers.

CHAPTER 7

CLOWNING AROUND

"No!" I yelled.

It was too late. Tula had made herself visible.

Bobby stopped screaming and smiled at Tula. "Hi," he said quietly. "Let's play."

Mom raised her head and frowned.

I held my breath.

Then she smiled. "Hi, Maria," she said to Tula. Tula smiled.

"It's Tula," Bobby said. But my mom didn't hear him, because she had customers.

I let my breath out. I had forgotten that Tula and Maria looked so much alike, with pink hair and striped outfits and clown makeup. Now I was glad I had let Tula paint her face. She was shorter than Maria, but Mom didn't notice the difference.

"That was lucky!" I hissed to Tula. "Now disappear!"

"Well, okay, Annie. But if I do, your brother will start screeching again," Tula warned.

"How can we get out of this?" I groaned.

"I will pretend to be a clown for a while," Tula whispered back. "No one will know."

I wasn't so sure, but it was too late to think of anything else. Mom finished selling apples and turned toward Tula. "Are you having a good time today?" she asked.

"Excellent," Tula said.

Mom frowned. "Your voice sounds different, Maria. I hope you're not catching a cold."

"*Catch,*" Tula said. "Trap. Capture." Her face wrinkled. "How do you capture the cold?"

Mom's frown got deeper. I had to think fast!

I laughed. "Maria's funny, isn't she?" I said. "What a joker!"

For a few seconds my mom acted confused. Then she asked Tula, "How's your ankle?"

"Excellent," Tula said again.

"Oh? I heard you twisted it in the race."

"It got better real fast," I said quickly. "Listen, Mom. I have to go tell fortunes, okay?"

"Sure, honey," Mom said. "Bye, Maria."

"Maybe you will," Tula said. "And maybe you won't."

I laughed real loud. "Oh, Maria, you're such

a clown," I said. Then I dragged Tula and Bobby away from the booth.

As soon as we were far enough away, Tula said, "How do you catch the cold?"

"You don't catch *the* cold," I said. "You catch *a* cold. You know. When you sneeze a lot and your nose runs."

"Your nose *runs?*" Tula felt her nose.

"Never mind," I said. "You have to go spy. Come on, Bobby."

"I want to stay with Tula," he said.

"Well, you can't," I told him.

Bobby looked as if he was going to yell again.

"I will take him with me, Annie," Tula said.

"Yes!" Bobby said.

"But then you'd have to stay visible," I said.

"Everyone will think I belong," Tula said. "Look around, Annie. No one who sees me is going begonias."

"Bananas," I said. But Tula was right. Nobody was staring at us. Everyone just thought she was another kid dressed like a clown.

"Okay," I said. "But can you watch Bobby and spy at the same time?"

"It will be as easy as cake," Tula said.

"Pie."

"Easy as pie. A piece of cake." Tula shook her head. "One of these days I will get it."

I started back to the fortune-telling booth. I saw Jason running toward the school and wondered what had happened *this* time.

When I got to my booth, the girl who was the fortune-teller told me everybody had asked for Madam Shasta. "They heard that some of your fortunes came true," she said. She handed me the scarves. "How do you do it?"

"It's a secret," I said mysteriously.

The girl left and one of Maria's cousins came in. I said I saw him splashing in waves in July.

"Really?" he said. "You're right. My whole family's going to the beach this summer. But I bet Maria said that, didn't she?"

"Not to me," I said. It was true. I'd only *heard* Maria talking about the beach.

Her cousin seemed to be impressed. After he left, Dawn came in.

"Kids are saying you can really tell fortunes," Dawn told me. "I don't believe it. I think you've just been lucky. I bet my fortune won't come true."

I knew I'd been lucky, but I wasn't going to admit it to Dawn. Instead, I decided to see if I could trick her into confessing to the sabotage. "Very strange," I said, rubbing the crystal ball.

Dawn snorted. "Okay, what do you see?"

"I see you walking on the schoolgrounds," I told her. "You're holding a small bottle."

"Huh?"

"You don't want anyone to see you," I said. "Now you're picking up a stick."

"A stick? What kind of fortune *is* this?" Dawn asked.

I stuck my face close to the ball. "Now you're opening the lid of the small bottle."

"What's in it?" Dawn asked.

"Something sticky," I said. "Very sticky."

"Wait a minute!" Dawn said. "I get it. You want me to say I put glue on your stupid baton."

I was embarrassed, but I didn't want her to know it. "I tell what I see," I said.

"Ha," Dawn said. "You can't see a thing. And you don't know anything, either!" She got up and stomped out of the booth.

A few minutes after Dawn left, Luis came into the booth. Where was Tula? Was she following Dawn? Or was she standing outside the booth, waiting for Luis to come out?

"Hi, Annie," Luis said. "Dawn told me what you said to her." He laughed. "Nice try."

"Do you want your fortune told or not?"

"Sure," he said. "Just don't think you can fool me into admitting anything."

I rubbed the crystal ball. "The picture is very clear," I said. "I see a lot of small, shiny cups." I leaned closer to the crystal. "Now I see a face. Aha!" I said. "It's Ms. Monroe. And she's handing little gold trophies out to her class."

Luis laughed. "Forget it, Annie. We have the contest in the bag." He left the booth laughing.

In the bag? Maybe Luis was just using an expression, but maybe he was hinting at something. Something about the sack race.

I got up and peeked out of the booth. I saw Luis walking away, but I didn't see Tula anywhere. She must be following Dawn, I thought. I wished I could tell Tula to go after Luis. If he *was* going to do something to the sacks, then she could catch him in the act!

I told three more fortunes. Then I was done for the day. I took off the scarves and left.

Tula wasn't around. If she was following Dawn, she was on the wrong trail. Bobby probably made her take him on the merry-go-round at least ten times. I decided to look there first.

I was hurrying past all the booths when I heard a voice call out, "Bobby!"

I knew that voice. But it wasn't Tula's voice. It was my mother's.

I turned toward it. It was Mom all right. She was in her booth, staring at Bobby and Tula.

"What are you doing here?" Mom asked Bobby. Then she asked Tula, "And where is Annie, Maria?"

Uh-oh, I thought. I was in big trouble.

CHAPTER 8

CLASSROOM CLUES

I ran over to the booth. "Hi, Mom," I said, extra cheerfully. Mom didn't smile.

"Annie!" she said. "*You* were supposed to watch your little brother. Not Maria." She smiled at Tula. "I'm sure you can take good care of him, Maria. But it was Annie's job."

Before I could think of an excuse, Tula said, "You're in a twist, aren't you, Mrs. Gibson?"

Mom stared at her.

"There she goes again!" I said to Mom. "Trying to be funny!" I poked Tula with my elbow. "Stop clowning around, Maria."

"It wasn't a joke," Tula said.

I jabbed her with my elbow again.

"It wasn't a very *good* joke," she said.

"Well," Mom said. "I suppose there's no harm done, but Annie, next time check with me before you ask someone else to look after Bobby. All right?"

"All right?" Tula said. Then *she* poked *me*.

"Ouch!" I said. "All right."

"I don't want to go with Annie," Bobby said.

"Thanks a lot," I said.

Mom laughed. "But, Bobby, we can't ask Maria to watch you all the time."

"She's not Maria," Bobby said. "She's a—"

"A clown!" I said quickly.

"Ha," Tula said.

I gave her a dirty look.

"I mean, ha, ha!" Tula laughed. "Don't worry, Mrs. Gibson. I'll watch Bobby."

"Okay, Mom?" I asked.

Mom said okay and gave us each a candy apple. Then I dragged Tula and Bobby away. "Tula, why did you go there?" I asked.

"I wanted an apple," Bobby said.

"So did I." Tula took a bite of hers. "Sticky, but delicious!" she said. "Annie, I followed Dawn after she came out of your booth. She ate four hot dogs. Then her face turned green. Was she ever mad!"

"Only trolls get green when they're mad," I told her. "People turn green when they're sick. After eating four hot dogs, Dawn probably had a stomachache," I explained. I was telling Tula about Luis when Sarah walked up to us.

"Hi, Annie," she said. "Hi, Maria." She looked at Tula. "Wait a second. You have green eyes. You're shorter than Maria, too."

"She's not Maria," Bobby said. "She's Tula."

"Tula?" Sarah said to me. "We don't know any Tula."

Tula giggled. I gave her a dirty look.

"She doesn't go to school here," I told Sarah. "She's just visiting with Bobby."

"Oh," Sarah said. "Hi, Tula. How come you're wearing a clown costume?"

"She isn't a clown. She's a troll," Bobby said.

"She doesn't look like a troll," Sarah said.

"She is a troll," Bobby said. "She *is!*"

Tula giggled. Sarah stared at her.

Uh-oh! I thought again.

Sarah just laughed. "Right. And I'm a wizard," she said to Bobby. "Come on, Annie, why don't we go play some of the other games? We could win a stuffed animal."

"If I put one more stuffed animal in my closet, my mom will kill me," I said. "Besides, I'm sort of baby-sitting."

Bobby and Tula both seemed to be insulted. I told Sarah I'd see her later, and she left.

I turned to Tula. "Here's what we'll do. I'll find Luis and keep an eye on him. You go to the equipment tent and keep an eye on the sacks. Then stay there. I'll come find you."

Tula went off with Bobby, and I started walking around, trying to find Luis. I saw Dawn and Tim and a bunch of other kids from Winslow's class at the Tower of Strength. But I didn't see Luis anywhere.

I decided to go to the tent where the ropes and sacks and stuff were kept. Maybe Tula had found something and was waiting for me.

To get to the tent, I had to pass by one of the school wings. All the windows were open. I was hurrying by when I heard Tula's voice.

"We have to find him, Bobby!" Tula said. "If we don't, we will be in a mountain of trouble!"

I ran to the door and went inside.

"I see him!" I heard Bobby say.

"Where?" Tula said.

Their voices were coming from my classroom! I went there and opened the door.

"Annie, no!" Tula cried. At the same time something small and brown ran over my foot. Harry the hamster scurried down the hall.

"Stop him!" Tula yelled.

Harry was fast, but I was faster. I caught up with him and picked him up. Then I went back to the classroom and put him in his cage.

"Tula, what are you and Bobby doing in here?" I said.

"I wanted to see Harry," Bobby said.

Bobby had met Harry on Open School Night.

Ever since then he was always begging Mom and Dad to get him a hamster. "Why did you let Bobby talk you into coming here?" I asked Tula. "You were supposed to wait at the equipment tent!"

"I did!" Tula said. "For a while."

"Not long enough," I told her. "Luis could be there right now, ruining our sacks."

"Then why aren't *you* there, Annie?" Tula asked. Her face was getting green. "You were supposed to find him!"

Tula was right, but I was still mad. Just then Bobby said, "What's this?"

I looked. Bobby was standing next to a desk, holding a jar out for me to see. I walked over and took it from him. It was a jar of petroleum jelly.

I peered inside the desk. There was Jason's little telescope. It still had some purple ink on one end. There was also a glue stick.

Suddenly it hit me.

"Tula, look!" I said. I held out the jar. "It's Vaseline. We don't use this stuff in class. Why do you suppose Jason has it in his desk?"

"For a joke?" Tula said. "You told me he likes to play sensible jokes on people."

"Practical jokes," I said. "But you're right. The grease on the rope and the glue on the baton—they're just the kinds of jokes Jason would play!

And I've seen him running into the school a lot, too. He must have been getting this stuff from his desk, and then putting it back."

Tula frowned. "But why would Jason want to make your team lose?"

"I don't know," I said. I thought a minute. "Jason was surprised when we lost the tug-of-war and the relay race. But if he sabotaged the stuff, then he wouldn't have been surprised. Unless he was just pretending."

"It's a puzzle," Tula said.

"And I can't ask him," I told her. "If he *did* do it, he would never admit it."

"If it's true, then you can trick him into telling you," Tula said.

"How?"

"Don't you remember what you said?" Tula asked. The green had faded from her face. "You said you wanted to pay Jason back for his jokes when you told his fortune."

"And you said you would help me," I said. "But I'm finished being the fortune-teller."

"You're not finished yet," Tula said. "I have a plan."

"What?"

"You'll see." Tula grinned. "Don't worry, Annie. It's going to be a piece of cake!"

CHAPTER 9

TROLL MAGIC

Before Tula and I went to the fortune-telling booth, we took Bobby back to my mom. Tula stayed visible so he wouldn't start yelling. I promised Bobby I'd take him on a ride later.

"Thank you for watching him, Maria," Mom said to Tula. "And take care of that cold."

Tula felt her nose. "It hasn't run away yet."

I pulled her away from the booth. "Your nose isn't going anywhere," I told her. "Now come on, let's go tell Jason's fortune."

A sixth grader was telling fortunes, and she didn't look too happy. Most of the sixth graders just wanted to hang out with their friends. They thought fortune-telling was dumb, so she was glad to let me take her place.

I popped the turban on my head and draped

some scarves over my shoulders. Then I waited at the door of the booth until I saw Jason.

He was walking along by himself, smiling. "Okay, Tula," I said. "Get ready."

Tula snapped her fingers. Now I was the only one who could see her.

Then I called out, "Hey, Jason. Have you had your fortune told yet?"

"I don't believe in that stuff," he said. "Nobody can tell the future."

"I can," I said.

He laughed. "Okay. Let's see you try."

Jason came in, and we sat down at the table. I rubbed the crystal ball. "I see danger ahead."

Jason laughed again. "What am I going to do, break a leg?" he asked.

"Not that kind of danger," I said. "I see a small gold cup. It might be a trophy." I rubbed the ball some more. "Someone's holding it, but I can't see who. And the cup has some letters on it. I see an *n* and an *o*."

"Winslow," Jason said. "Or Monroe. That means the contest could go either way."

"Yes, but I told you I saw danger," I said. "And since I'm telling your fortune, that can only mean one thing. The Monroe team is in danger of losing."

"I know that already, Annie," Jason said.

"You can't tell what's going to happen. This fortune stuff is a joke." He stood up.

"Wait! I really do have special powers."

"Oh, sure," Jason said. "So prove it."

"Sit down," I told him.

Jason sat down.

"Look around the booth," I said. "Who do you see?"

"This is crazy," Jason said. But he looked around. "Okay. I see you and me. We're the only ones in here."

"Are you sure?" I asked.

Jason looked under the table. "Nobody here," he said.

"Do you see any wires or ropes?"

"Nothing." He sat back up. "Come on, Annie. What's the joke?"

"It's no joke," I said. "Watch!"

Jason just laughed.

Tula, who was standing behind me, took the scarves off my shoulders.

"Hey!" Jason said.

Tula started waving the scarves around. I could see her, but Jason couldn't. To him, it looked as if the scarves were waving through the air by themselves.

"Hey!" Jason said again. "How are you doing that?"

I didn't answer him. I was trying too hard not to laugh.

Tula twirled the scarves around a little more. Then she draped them back on me. Next, she picked up the crystal ball. She held it over her head and slowly walked around the booth.

Jason's mouth was open. He couldn't take his eyes off the ball.

Finally Tula lowered the ball back to the table. Jason must have thought it was floating down. "How did you do that?" he asked, checking again for wires or ropes.

"Magic," I said. "Now do you believe that I have special powers?"

"Uh," Jason said. "I—I guess so."

"Good. Then I'll look into your future." I rubbed the crystal ball and stared into it. "I see you, Jason," I said. "You have a small jar with you. It has Vaseline in it. You're walking toward a yellow rope."

"That's not my future!" Jason said. "That's my past!"

"Then you *did* do it!" I said. "You greased the rope and you glued the baton."

"Okay, okay!" Jason said. "I did it."

"But why?" I asked. "Why did you sabotage your own team?"

"I wasn't trying to," he said. "I was trying to do it to Winslow's team. But they grabbed the clean side of the rope first, and I couldn't do anything about it. And then before the relay race, I saw Mrs. Winslow holding a baton. I thought it was her team's, so I waited until she left and I glued it. But—"

"But you glued the wrong one!" I said.

"I know," Jason said, embarrassed. "But they're only one race ahead of us. We'll be even if we win the sack race. And we will!"

"Jason, did you do something to the sacks?" I asked. "You did, didn't you?"

Jason nodded.

"What?"

"I sneaked into school and got my scissors. Then I unraveled the bottoms of some of the Winslow sacks a little bit," he said.

"How do you know they're the Winslow sacks?" I asked. "They're all the same. Brown burlap, like potato sacks."

"I know, but I put the bad ones in a separate pile," Jason said. "So all I have to do is make sure Sarah takes the others. That's where I was going before you dragged me in here. Then when Winslow's Wimps start hopping, their feet will get all tangled up in the loose threads. But nobody will be able to tell it was sabotage. They'll lose and we'll win!"

"Sure," I said. "Just like we won the relay

race and the tug-of-war. Your sack trick could backfire, too."

"I guess you're right."

"So, go get rid of the sacks you fixed," I told him. "Put good ones in their places."

"I can't," Jason said. "Somebody might see me. I was lucky nobody saw me before."

Behind me, Tula said, "No one would see *me*, Annie."

"Right!" I said. "No one would see you."

"Yes, they would," Jason said.

"Not you," I told him.

"Huh?"

"I'll go now, Annie," Tula said. "And don't worry—I will take care of everything!"

"Great!" I said.

"What's great?" Jason said.

Tula left.

"Okay," I said to Jason. "Now that you believe in my special powers, I will tell you what is going to happen." I rubbed the crystal ball and looked into it. "I see the people lining up for the third-grade sack race. Both teams are pulling the sacks over their legs. Now they're hopping. And nobody's feet are getting tangled. The sacks are all fine."

"Are you sure?" Jason asked doubtfully.

"Of course I'm sure," I told him. "Madam Shasta knows all."

CHAPTER 10

AND THE WINNERS ARE . . .

When Jason and I got to the field, there was only about a minute left before the sack race. Both teams were already at the starting line.

"It's about time you got here!" Kelly said to us. "Where have you been?"

"What difference does it make?" I said. I didn't see Tula anywhere.

I ran over to Sarah. "Did you check the sacks before you handed them out?" I asked.

"Yes," she said. "They look fine. What could somebody do to a sack, anyway?" She handed me one and got ready to race.

I almost told her about Jason. But I changed my mind. He felt bad, I could tell. And even though he'd tried to cheat, it hadn't worked. It had hurt his own team. I didn't think he'd be playing any of his practical jokes for a while.

I checked my sack before I pulled it on. No loose threads. But maybe I just had a good one.

I looked for Tula again. I saw someone with pink hair run to the starting line and step into a sack. But then I saw the orange stripe in the hair. It was Maria, not Tula. Maria's ankle must be okay, I thought. She was in such a hurry, she didn't take her clown suit off.

I took a deep breath and crossed my fingers that Tula had gotten rid of the bad sacks. Then I crossed my fingers that our team would win. Then Ms. Monroe blew the whistle, and the two third grades took off hopping.

At first Sarah and Jason were way ahead, but behind them was a bunch of Winslow kids. Behind them was most of the Monroe team, including me. If enough of us didn't catch up, we could kiss the Field-Day contest goodbye.

Suddenly two Winslow kids fell down. By the time they got up, Sam and Kelly had passed them. Then Dawn fell down and Maria passed her. Now we were in the lead.

I could see Luis ahead of me. If I could just catch up and pass him, we'd win the race.

Luis was chubby, but fast. He didn't look as if he would ever fall down. The race was up to me, and I didn't think I could catch him.

Then I heard Tula's voice. "Come on,

Annie!" she shouted. "You can beat that moss-brain, easy as pie!"

I looked toward the finish line. There was Tula, jumping up and down. Her pink hair was flopping back and forth, and she was waving her arms like crazy.

Then I saw Mom and Bobby at the finish line, too. I guess someone had taken over the candy apple booth for Mom so she could watch. She was staring at Maria, who was still hopping.

"Hurry, Annie!" Tula shouted. "Catch the moss-brain!"

Then Mom stopped watching Maria and turned to Tula!

All of a sudden I remembered. Trolls sometimes become visible when they get excited. Tula was more excited than ever. Now that my mom could see her and Maria so close together, I knew she'd start asking questions!

Mom gazed at Maria, then at Tula. Even from where I was, I could see her frown.

I started hopping faster. I had to get to the finish line so I could tell Tula to disappear.

Mom looked at Tula and then at Maria.

I hopped even faster. "Tula!" I shouted. It was hard to yell and hop at the same time, but I did it. "Tula, vanish!"

"Why don't *you* vanish?" Luis yelled. He

was hopping right next to me. I'd caught up to him! I tried to go faster.

"Come on, Annie!" Tula hollered.

Mom was looking at Maria now.

"Tula, disappear!" I screamed.

"Oh! *Erks!*" Tula snapped her fingers.

Mom whirled around to where Tula had been. When she didn't see her, she looked around the crowd of kids who'd already finished the race. Boy, was she confused!

I didn't see Luis anymore. I glanced over my shoulder. He was only a couple of feet behind me. I had hopped so fast, I'd passed him!

Sarah and Jason were already over the finish line. So were two other kids from our class. They were all screaming at me to hurry.

Sam crossed the finish line. Then Maria did. Luis was so close behind me, I could hear him huffing and puffing. I had a few feet to go.

I gritted my teeth, hopped as fast as I could, and crossed the finish line about two seconds ahead of Luis. I plopped down on the ground right in front of Tula. "Thanks, Tula!" I gasped. "You saved the race. Your plan was great!"

Tula gave me a stubby thumbs-up.

Everybody on my team ran over to me. Sarah and even Kelly hugged me. Jason pounded me on the shoulder. "Nice going,

Annie!" he said. Then he whispered, "How did you know the sacks would be okay?"

"Magic," I whispered back.

Mom and Bobby came over and told me I was great. Maria was standing next to me, and Mom smiled at her. "You were great, too, Maria," she said. "It's so strange. While you were hopping along, I saw somebody watching the race. And she looked exactly like you. Pink wig and everything. She was shouting at Annie." Mom looked at me. "Something about moss and brains."

Bobby giggled. "That was—"

"Just another kid dressed like a clown," I said quickly.

"I guess so," Maria said.

"Your cold sounds better already," my mother said to Maria. "And thanks again for watching Bobby."

"For *what*?" Maria said. I took her arm and pulled her away. "See you later, Mom," I said.

"Annie, what was your mother talking about?" Maria asked. "I don't have a cold. And I wasn't watching your brother."

"Nothing," I said. "It's just a case of mistaken identity."

"Huh?"

"Never mind," I said.

*   *   *

Soon it was time for the big popcorn count. As everybody gathered around the big, see-through bin, Tula said, "Annie! I can see daylight!"

I thought she meant Dawn, but then she said, "At home, in the Land of the Trolls! I can only stay a few more seconds. But I want to see who wins the popcorn contest."

"It won't take very long," I said. I wanted her to see who won, too.

"I hope not," Sam said. He was standing on one side of me and thought I was talking to him. "Keep your fingers crossed that Mrs. Kupperman doesn't make a speech," he whispered.

Mrs. Kupperman, the principal, was standing next to the bin. "All right, everybody," she said. "The correct number is: ten thousand, five hundred and ten pieces of popcorn."

I could hardly believe it. Tula's number was right if you subtract the fifty-one pieces she ate! And anyhow the number was so high that fifty pieces more or less didn't matter.

"I told you, Annie!" Tula said to me. "Close en*counters* always works!"

I smiled at her. Sarah, who was standing right behind Tula, smiled back at me.

"First, we'll start with the kindergarten winner," Mrs. Kupperman said.

"Ten seconds. Then I have to go!" Tula said.

Mrs. Kupperman checked with the kindergarten teachers. They gave her the winning number for that grade. It was fifty-one.

Everybody in my class was nervous. This was our chance to break the tie with the Winslow team and win the Field Day contest.

"Eight seconds!" Tula said.

"What number did you guess, Annie?" Maria asked me.

"I didn't make a guess," I told her. "But I have a prediction to make," I announced.

Everybody turned to me.

I used my fortune-teller voice. "I predict that Sarah will come closest to the right number."

"I hope you're right, Annie," Sarah said.

"Me, too," I told her.

Luis, who was standing near us, laughed. "Not a chance," he said.

"Wait and see," I said. I crossed my fingers.

"Five seconds!" Tula said.

Finally it was time for the third-grade winner to be announced. "The closest guess is ten thousand. From Sarah O'Dell in Ms. Monroe's class!" Mrs. Kupperman said.

"Yesss!" Jason said, and we all cheered. We had won the Field Day contest!

"We did it, Tula!" I said. Everybody was still cheering, so they didn't hear me. "We won!"

"Yesss!" Tula said. "And now, I have to go, Annie! If I don't, I'll be in a mountain of trouble!"

"Will you come back?"

"Of course." Tula laughed her squeaky laugh. "All I have to do is say the magic words."

"Goodbye, Annie," she said. She snapped her stubby fingers and said, *"Shamaz-Shamat!"* Then she disappeared.

"Goodbye, Tula," I said, even though she couldn't hear me anymore.

I glanced around me. Everyone in my class was still screaming and slapping hands.

"Who's number one?" Jason yelled.

"Monroe's Miracles!" Sam shouted.

Kelly smiled at Dawn. Dawn didn't smile back.

Maria and Sarah were jumping up and down. Luis and Tim just stood there. For once, they weren't acting like moss-brains. They even congratulated us.

Sarah ran up to me. "How did you know I'd get so close?" she asked.

"Yeah, Annie," Jason said. "How'd you get your special powers?"

I wished I could say I had help from a troll. But who would believe me? So I just laughed and said, "Madam Shasta knows all."

ABOUT THE AUTHOR
AND ILLUSTRATOR

CAROL ELLIS is the author of over twenty books for young readers, including *There's a Troll in My Popcorn*, and the best-selling *Camp Fear*, *The Window*, and *The Stepdaughter*. Carol Ellis lives in New York with her husband and son.

PAT PORTER has illustrated over twenty-five children's books, including *There's a Troll in My Popcorn*, *Slime Time*, *Luke's Bully*, and *Blue Tree Red Sky*, by Norma Klein. She has lived in New York for over 30 years.